Marie Léonard

Illustrated by Andrée Prigent

Tibili

The

Little Boy

Who Didn't

Want to Go

to School

Kane/Miller
BOOK PUBLISHERS

First American Edition 2002 by Kane/Miller Book Publishers
La Jolla, California

Originally published in France in 1996 under the title
Tibili, le petit garçon qui ne voulait pas aller à l'école
by Éditions Magnard

Library of Congress Cataloging-in-Publication Data
Léonard, Marie.
[Tibili, le petit garçon qui ne voulait pas aller à l'école. English]
Tibili, the little boy who didn't want to go to school/Marie Léonard, Andrée Prigent
—1st Amer. ed. p.cm.
Summary: After Tibili, a young African boy, follows Crope the spider's suggestion as to
how he can avoid starting school, he discovers he wants to go after all.
ISBN 1-929132-20-4
[1. First day of school–Fiction. 2. Reading–Fiction. 3. Animals–Fiction 4.
Blacks–Africa–Fiction. 5. Africa–Fiction.] I. Title; Tibili. II. Prigent, Andrée, ill. III. Title.
PZ7.L5495Ti2001   [E]–dc21   2001038793

Printed and bound in Singapore by Tien Wah Press Pte. Ltd.
1 2 3 4 5 6 7 8 9 10

Tibili
is a happy
little boy
who laughs
all the time,
morning
to night.

Sometimes,
if he is not
too tired from
playing all day,
he even laughs
himself to sleep.

The only
time he stops
laughing is when
he eats or when
he braids his
sister's hair.
Kablé likes to
look pretty
and Tibili's small
fingers are just
the right size
for braiding.

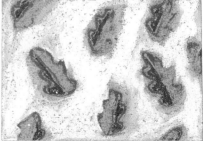

One day Tibili's mother tells him he'll be going to school when classes start next year.

Tibili stops laughing.

He doesn't
want to go to school.

He doesn't want to sit in a classroom,
in front of a boring old chalkboard.

Tibili doesn't think he needs to know
how to read and write.

He would rather read like his grandfather,
not from a piece of paper,
but from the sky, where the sun sings
during the day and the moon
dances during the night.

He would rather read from the red dust that covers the road, where a thousand colorful animals come and go every which way, without ever going to school.

He would
rather dream
that he is
trying to catch
a barracuda
(a big one like this)
or riding a
gazelle racing
at full speed, or
swinging with
the monkeys
in the forest.

Tibili doesn't want to wear a white uniform. If he wore it to the beach no one could see him on the sand. Someone might step on him.

Tibili is very sad.

He worries, like
the shepherds'
thin buffalo,
always looking
for food.

What can he do?

How can he get out of going to school?

Moons pass one after the other, and the beginning of the school year is getting closer and closer.

Tibili asks
Pi-ou the
lizard,

*"What can I
do so I won't
have to go
to school?"*

"You could hide in the trunk of the breadfruit tree," answers Pi-ou.

Tibili thinks he could hide for awhile – but not every day!

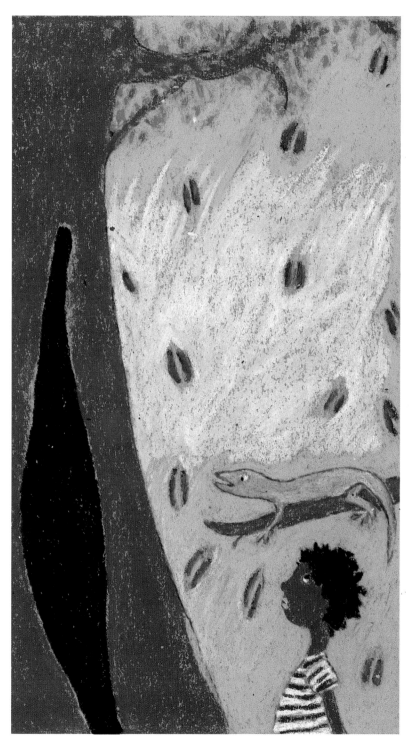

He talks to Koumi, the bat,
who is resting on his branch.

Koumi tells him,
*"When the day comes to start school,
you could stay in bed and
say that you are sick."*

Tibili thinks.

He can't say he is sick every day.

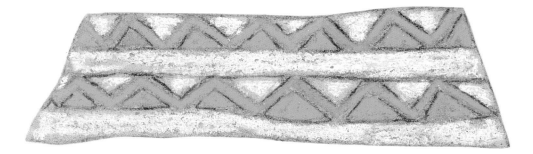

Besides, he likes to tell the truth.

Finally he goes to see Crope, the spider, who always seems to know everything.

Crope tells him: *"I can only think of one solution. Go find the Box of Knowledge. It's buried close to the bend of the river, between the papaya and the tamarind trees."*

"There you will see a big reddish stone. Roll it over and dig in the ground until you find something very hard. That will be the Box of Knowledge.

Take it out with great care. Open it, and you will find what you are looking for."

Tibili runs as fast as he can toward the bend of the river. He rolls the stone he finds away, digs in the ground between the papaya and the tamarind trees and finds something very hard.

It's the Box!
He tries to open it, but he can't.

Kut-Kut, the mischievous guinea hen, asks him from her perching place, "*What are you doing, Tibili?*"

"*I'm trying to open the Box of Knowledge.*"

"*Oh, that's easy, silly. Just read the directions on the bottom.*"

Tibili turns the Box over,
then lowers his head and says nothing.

"Well?" asks Kut-Kut.

"I…I…can't read," replies Tibili.

"You can't read?"
laughs Kut-Kut.

"He can't read!"
she shouts, so everyone can hear.

"He can't read!"
the other guinea hens repeat.

"He can't read!"
answers back the echo.

Tibili quickly
puts the Box
back in its
hiding place,
covers it
with soil,
rolls the
stone back
into place
and leaves.

When the guinea hens can't see him, Tibili runs home as fast as he can and asks his Mom just one question:

"Is school starting soon?"